The True Story of World Champion Surfer
Layne Beachley

Written By
Chloe Chick

Illustrated By
Natalie Kwee

Edited By
Rachel Jacqueline

WS Education

NEW JERSEY · LONDON · SINGAPORE · BEIJING · SHANGHAI · HONG KONG · TAIPEI · CHENNAI · TOKYO

Chloe:
For Jimmy J McKay

. . . .

Natalie:
For those who
helped me get tough
when things got rough

Published by

WS Education, an imprint of
World Scientific Publishing Co. Pte. Ltd.

5 Toh Tuck Link, Singapore 596224
USA office: 27 Warren Street, Suite 401-402, Hackensack, NJ 07601
UK office: 57 Shelton Street, Covent Garden, London WC2H 9HE

Library of Congress Cataloging-in-Publication Data
Names: Chick, Chloe, author. | Kwee, Natalie, illustrator.
Title: Brave Beachley : the true story of world champion surfer Layne Beachley
　/ written by Chloe Chick ; illustrated by Natalie Kwee.
Description: New Jersey : World Scientific, 2015.
Identifiers: LCCN 2015035154 | ISBN 9789814713993 (hardcover)
Subjects: LCSH: Beachley, Layne, 1972- | Surfers--Australia--Biography.
Classification: LCC GV838.B384 C55 2015 | DDC 797.3/2092--dc23
LC record available at http://lccn.loc.gov/2015035154

BRAVE BEACHLEY
The True Story of Professional Surfer Layne Beachley

For photocopying of material in this volume, please pay a copying fee through the Copyright Clearance Center, Inc., 222 Rosewood Drive, Danvers, MA 01923, USA. In this case permission to photocopy is not required from the publisher.

ISBN 978-981-4713-99-3

Printed in Singapore

SISUGIRLS

SisuGirls is a global movement inspiring and encouraging girls to be brave, confident and strong. Sisu is a Finnish term for determination, bravery and resilience. We want all girls to have the self-belief and conviction to try new things, the tenacity to endure and the bravery to push boundaries.

Brave Beachley is the second book in our collection of stories about courageous females.

Proceeds from the sale of *Brave Beachley* go to the SisuGirls movement and the Layne Beachley Aim for the Stars Foundation.

Thank you for supporting SisuGirls.

www.sisugirls.org

I grew up in Australia,
    across from Manly Beach,
    with sun and sand and water,
    all within my reach.

The beach was in my culture,
where my friends and I would play.
Long days down at the surf club,
soaking up a summer's day.

One day the weather darkened,
    the sun refused to show its face.
I was only six years old
    when my dear Mum left this place.

When sadness like that happens,
words cannot express the pain.
The key was finding small things,
to bring sun instead of rain.

I found my
joy in water,

I would dive and
splash and swim.

8

Jumping through
the swirling waves,

my back like a
dolphin's fin.

And then I got a *surfboard*,
    it was big and soft so I could learn —
paddling, standing, gliding,
    and one day, I would turn.

The first time I rode a wave,
I was swallowed with a thump!
I swirled under the water,
in a solid, sandy dump.

My Dad would often tell me:
"Don't worry, you'll be right!
Sometimes little knocks like that
are nothing but a fright."

"Now up you hop, onto your feet,
    and give a little more,
    look ahead, do not look down,
        aim your board right for the shore."

And before I knew it, there I was,
standing high up on a crest,
surfing down a wave face screaming:
"THIS IS JUST THE BEST!"

"I have a dream," I shouted,
"I am certain and I know,
I want to be a surfer, I want to be a pro!"

But the surfer boys at Manly snorted:
"Dreams like that are not for you.
Can a girl really be a surfer?
A professional surfer too?"

When I looked around my sandy kingdom,
there were no other girls in sight.
I was the only one braving big waves,
I thought: "Maybe those boys were right."

But then I changed my mindset:
      "Layne, you're tough right to your core,
you are brave and determined,
          you can do this — that's for sure...

...Get out there and surf the big waves,
show them how it's done!
Go and chase your vision
of becoming number one."

But first I had to work hard,
to make my dreams come true.
Surfing,
working,
training,
dedication through and through.

You see, being the best doesn't just happen,
you must work steadily towards your dream.
And the harder you work each day,
the closer it will seem.

Sometimes the ocean would scare me,
the water deep and cold and strong.
But once I told myself *"I'm brave"*,
I wasn't scared for very long.

Pushing through the breaks, I'd paddle,
then wait until the swell was building high.
Quickly, I'd turn and face the shoreline, and say,
"You can do this Layne, just try."

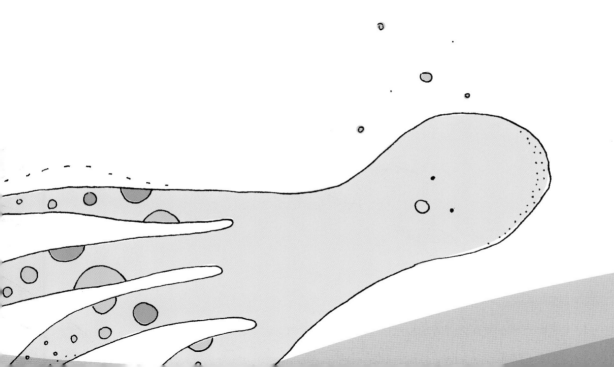

I became the world surfing champion,
seven times, the female best!
I persevered, I never quit,
I had passed my ultimate test.

One of my greatest surfing memories
was catching waves in Jeffreys Bay.
Waiting in the water
for the swell to turn my way.

Before I had a chance to
catch my wave and surf to shore,
around me were 30 dolphins...
...Perhaps a couple more.

It was little moments like these
that sent shivers down my spine.
They rewarded and reminded me:
My dreams were truly, wonderfully mine.

It's about fighting for your passions,
always giving it your all.
Setting goals and catching dreams,
and getting up after a fall.

Because tough times are sure to happen,
they are part and parcel of life's plan.

But don't let those tough times stop you,
pick yourself up and say: *"I CAN!"*

It is just what I am thinking
when I am flying down a wave...

...I tell myself,
"Come on Layne, you can do this!
You are tough and strong and brave!"

Layne Beachley AO is a former professional surfer from Manly, Australia . She won the World Championship seven times and is one of Australia's greatest athletes.

Born in 1972 and given up for adoption by her 17-year-old mother, Layne lost her adoptive mother when she was just six. As a 16-year-old, Layne made her debut on the ASP Women's World Tour and, by the time she was 20, she was ranked number 6 in the world. In 1998, Layne's determination and focus paid off and she achieved the first of six consecutive world titles.

For the first eight years of her surfing career, Layne predominantly supported herself, working up to four jobs at any one time. In 2003, with the desire to prevent other young women from having to endure the same hardship, she established the Aim for the Stars Foundation with the goal to encourage, motivate and provide for all aspiring women. Inspired by its motto "Dare To Dream, Pursue your Passion and Aspire to Achieve", the foundation to date has provided over 450 girls with financial and moral support in areas such as music, science, culture, arts and sport.

The constant in all of the above is the conviction that there are no boundaries when it comes to realising one's potential.

. . . .

www.laynebeachley.com
www.aimforthestars.com.au